The Adventures of Border Bob

"My little dog – a heartbeat at my feet."

Edith Wharton

Border Bob

Border Bob lives in a kennel at the side of the Big House.

The Big House is situated close to the Tweed, which is a river that runs along the border between England and Scotland, from where Border Bob gets his name.

Bob is a Border Terrier.

He is a small, curious and friendly dog with a biscuit-coloured coat and a wise little face. He has a keen nose and he is very feisty - he loves to chase the rats that lurk around the horse barn and he has a special dislike of Reynard, the fox who lives in a secret den in the nearby woods. Reynard likes to steal away the chickens from the coop and Bob always tries to stop him. Bob is ready to give Reynard what for if he ever catches him.

But mostly, when he is not busy guarding the big house or chasing foxes, Border Bob likes to sit at the door of his cosy little kennel with his chin on his paws and watch the world go by.

In the border country, winter comes early, the days are short and the nights are long and dark. From late September, the air turns chilly, the wind blows hard and by mid-October the frost begins to hang in the air. When it snows, Bob likes to run around and burrow into the chilly white stuff.

One evening, the Big Man, who lives in the Big House, saw Bob running around in the snow chasing and biting at the snowflakes that were falling, and shouted 'Come inside Bob!' and with one large hand he scooped up Bob and carried him inside and dried him off with a warm, soft towel. So that evening, the first night of a particularly long and harsh winter, Bob lay in front of a roaring fire, between the Big Man's two huge Irish Wolfhounds, Brian and Boru. The wolfhounds didn't mind Bob because he was friendly and feisty, and he didn't take up much room.

But mostly, on even the coldest winter nights, Bob was happy to lie in his kennel because it was cosy and safe. He has an old warm blanket in his kennel that was given to him by The Girl, who is the daughter of the Big Man from the Big House. The girl's name is Celia.

Bob loves Celia the most.

Celia calls Bob 'Border Bear' because she says he looks like a little bear, and whenever Celia returns home from school for a visit she calls out *"Bobbeeeee"* and when he runs and leaps up to lick her face she pets him and hugs him. While she is at home she takes him for walks every day, and she always has treats for him.

Celia gave Bob his kennel blanket and it has her special scent on it and Bob loves his blanket because, although he loves all the people in the Big House (even Mrs. Hands the Cook), he loves Celia the most.

Every morning Bob peeps from his kennel to see if it a good day, then he steps out and takes a good sniff of the air, to see what is going on in the world - his nose is more powerful than his sight, even more powerful than his keen ears - then he goes into the stable and gets a breakfast of kibbles from

Stan the stable boy. He watches as Stan feeds and mucks out the horses in the stable, and Stan always has time to stop and pet Bob. Stan will take an apple from his pocket and crunch it, and he always says the same thing, 'An apple a day, Bob. An apple a day.'

Sometimes Hooks the Butler, the man who runs the Big House, gives Bob scraps of food from the back-kitchen door. Bob loves to eat beef in gravy or chicken or a plate of pie. He doesn't eat carrots or sprouts (yukk!) though he enjoys a piece of Yorkshire pudding. When Bob has eaten the scraps that Butler gives him, he likes to sneak into the kitchen and lie contentedly in the corner to enjoy the lovely smells and watch the people bustling about. And to spot if any more scraps of food fall onto the floor, where he will quickly snaffle them up. But if Mrs. Hands the Cook sees him, she scolds him and tells him that dogs are not allowed in the kitchen. Then he goes back to his cosy kennel and puts his chin on his paws and watches the world go by.

On afternoons Bob likes to go to the Garden and accompany Old Tom the gardener as he tends to the strawberries and the pea pods. The Garden has a large wall round it with a single wooden door through which Old Tom wheels his barrow back and forwards. Bob likes to watch Old Tom and see what he is doing with the plants and the fruit. Sometimes Bob will chase a butterfly or a spider. But he never manages to catch them. Bob's kennel is tucked into the side of the Big House, near the kitchen door, right by the path to the stables, so he gets to see everything that goes on around him. He can also see the chicken coop and he protects the squawking chickens from Mr. Reynard, the sneaky old fox.

Mr. Reynard is a very old fox, and wise to the ways of the world, so Bob has to work very hard to stop him from stealing the chickens. 'This is your Main Job,' Celia told Bob while he was still a little puppy. 'You must protect the chickens and keep them safe from that horrid fox.' So of course, Bob takes this job very seriously. Mostly, however, his job is to keep the Big House clear of small creatures like mice and rats, and also to bark when visitors come, and also to chase Wee Jock, the postman who delivers the mail. Bob does this job very well.

Bob and the Hejog.

Border Bob is very proud of the fact that he chases away the rats and mice and little creatures who live beneath the floorboards and in the eaves of the barn. When Bob sees a rat or a small creature, his tail points upwards and he gives chase. Fortunately for these creatures, Bob also barks very loudly before he begins to chase, so they usually have time to scramble down their little holes and hide while Bob patrols back and forward, panting and sniffing the air for their scent.

On one occasion in the early summer however, Bob saw a strange, slow-moving Rat with prickly-looking fur, and when he barked and gave chase, the creature simply curled up and sat still. Furious, Bob tried to bite it, but its fur was sharp and it stung Bob's mouth, so he yelped in surprise and jumped back, then, when the prickly rat did not move, Bob barked and jumped forward and bit again. This time his lips were prickled so he yelped and jumped back, then he barked and leaped forward again. And again. And again. Every time he bit, his mouth was prickled, and this made him even more feisty.

This went on for some time and Bob was beginning to think he wasn't very easily winning this argument, but Bob is a feisty dog and he doesn't always know when to give up, so it was only when Stan the stableboy saw what was happening and came over and picked up Bob that the argument between Bob and the prickly rat ended. Stan carried Bob into the barn, laughing, 'That's not a rat,' Stan said, 'That's a hedgehog, and you can't bite them.'

In reply, Bob wriggled in Stan's arms and tried to lick his face. Stan carried Bob to the stone trough just inside the barn and gently washed Bob's mouth with fresh water and a clean handkerchief. This chore completed, Bob felt better, and he allowed Stan to take him into the yard, set him down and put on his collar and leash. Then they walked back outside into the sunshine. Bob growled when he saw the prickly rat walking slowly across the front drive, but Stan petted him and told him he was a good boy and to leave such creature alone, so Bob calmed down and was a good boy. He sat and watched the strange creature. What did Stan call it?, a Hejog, and thought, well, if it isn't a rat then maybe I shan't need to bite it. And also, it's not hiding beneath the barn so I don't need to chase it. Otherwise I might just give it what for. Just for good measure, Bob gave another bark as the hedgehog disappeared into the long grass and Stan laughed again, 'You saw it off, eh Bob?' Stan said, 'You saw off the Hejog.'

Bob wagged his tail.

He'd seen off the Hejog.

And for the rest of the day he felt very proud of himself as he sat at his kennel, with his chin resting on his paws, watching the world go by and keeping an eye on things.

Bob's cousin Bingley

The Big Man was in charge of the house and he owned all the land for miles around, even as far as the river. Bob loved the Big Man but he was a tiny bit scared of him too, because the

Big Man was fierce when he shouted. He was fierce when he laughed too, which made Bob very happy, but that didn't happen too often, so Bob always wanted to do the right thing in case the Big Man would give him a pet and say nice words. One day Bob heard the sound of a motor car approaching the Big House, and he could smell the stink of the engine which, as it approached, was smoking and making barking noises. Bob barked in return. The car stopped at the end of the drive and a man got out, followed by a small brown dog. Bob approached and sniffed the dog and the man bent down and petted Bob and then the other dog, which he called Bingley. Bob wasn't sure he liked the man, but he liked being petted, and he was curious about this other dog, Bingley. He looked up when he heard the front door of the Big House open, and the Big Man came striding out, shouting 'Hello, Tam!' to the man who had arrived in the car.

'Morning Alistairrrr,' the man said in return, making a strange sound at the end of his words.

'I see you've met Bob,' the Big Man said, bending down to stroke Bob's ear.

'Aye, he's a fine beastie,' Tam said.

Bob decided he didn't like being a beastie.

'He's a cousin of Bingley, I believe,' Tam continued, 'They share the same grandmother.'

'Aye. Well come on in,' the Big Man said, 'You can tell me what's going on out there in the world.'

Bob turned and sniffed Bingley again. Bingley sniffed him in return. Bob decided they could be friends. He turned and trotted toward the stables and Bingley followed, stopping to smell the fence where the chicken coop was. The chickens clucked but Bingley ignored them and went to follow Bob into the stables. Bob showed him where the cosy parts of the stables were. He showed him the horses. Bingley wasn't afraid of the horses and neither was Bob because Border Terriers are bred to run with horses and sometimes, when the day is long and the little legs of a border terrier get tired they get a lift in the rider's saddle bag. But this day, Bob and Bingley were only having a look around. The horses glanced down at them but mostly ignored them. The horses were huge, they were well bred and well fed and cared for by Stan the stableboy, and the Big Man said they were the best steeplechasers in the county. When Bingley went too close to the water trough of one particularly big horse the horse nosed him away and made a horsey sound.

Bob took Bingley to the kitchen door, and Grace, Mrs. Hand's kitchen assistant, came out gave them a bowl of scraps to share. Then Bob showed Bingley where the trees were down by the stream where they sniffed around for the scent of rats or foxes, though they didn't find any. Altogether it was a good morning and Bob was proud of doing his job.

Eventually, Bob and Bingley heard a whistle and they both trotted to the source, back at the front door of the Big House. Tam and the Big Man were back at the car. Tam was asking, 'You sure you won't rejoin the hunt? Your horses are built for the chase, and yon wee beastie would make a fine dog for going to ground.'

The Big Man smiled, 'I've done enough hunting, Tam.'

'You should think about getting Bob blooded.'

The Big Man shook his head, 'I saw enough blood in the war, Tam. No need to see any more. And as I said, Bob isn't a working dog, he's Celia's pet. I got him when...' all of a sudden the Big Man fell silent.

Tam shuffled his feet for a moment and nothing was said, then quietly he said, 'Aye, alrrright then Alistair,' adding, 'I'll say no more.'

'But if the hunt passes Craigmorley House, feel free to drop in for a wee dram,' the Big Man said. Bob knew that Craigmorley was the name of the Big House.

'Aye, I will do, I will do.' Bob could tell Tam was happy by the tone of his voice.

Tam climbed into his car, and Bingley followed, jumping across into the passenger seat where he sat, very proud. Bob thought that if he were in a car he would be proud too. Tam started the engine and the noise and smell was overpowering to Bob and he wrinkled his nose, but Bingley sat proudly waiting for the car to pull away. The Big Man said, 'Give my regards to Mary and the boys.'

'I will,' Tam said. 'Give my love to that wonderful daughter of yours.'

The Big Man nodded and watched as the car pulled away then, with a single wave, turned and walked back into the house. Bob watched Bingley and Tam drive along the drive until they were out of sight. Then he trotted happily back to the kitchen in the search for food.

Later that day the Big Man came out to the stables and told Stan to saddle up Mercy, his favourite black mare. He mounted the mare and set out into the countryside with Bob at his heels. Horse and dog trotted at first, but then the Big Man let Mercy have her head and they galloped together for miles through the fields and bracken, through copse and wood, leaping streams and gates (Bob ran fearlessly through the freezing streams and darted swiftly between the bars of the gates).

By late afternoon when returned home, Bob was covered in mud and brambly twigs, and he was a little bit tired. He watched as Stan took the reins and saw to Mercy, while the Big Man strode silently back to the house.

When Stan had cleaned and fed Mercy he gave Bob a bowl of food he collected from the kitchen, then freshened his water bowl from the standpipe. 'You did well today, Bob,' Stan said, brushing him thoroughly after he'd tended to Mercy. 'There's not many can keep up with Mercy when Lord Alistair lets her run free.' He patted Bob on the head with affection and rubbed his shoulders kindly. Then he stood up and set about sweeping out the stables as Bob watched him from the doorway.

Bob felt very proud.

Bob meets Mr.Fox

The Big House is actually called Craigmorley House, and it is set in the Border region, between England and Scotland. Over many centuries armies from England and Scotland have made war with each other and the border between these two ancient lands has moved back and forward many times, depending on whose army won the most recent battle. Craigmorley House has belonged to both England and Scotland at different times in its long history.

This land between two countries, where Craigmorley House is set, is now simply known as 'the Borders' because no one really knows where England ends and Scotland begins, or vice versa; some people on the borders speak with an English voice, other people, who might live right next door, speak with a soft Scottish accent. Because of its long history of battle and marauding armies, and because it is remote from the rest of the world, there aren't a lot of people living in the Borders, but the people who do live in the Borders are hardy and independent. Just like Bob. And just how hardy Bob really was became apparent in the days that horrible Mr. Reynard Fox tried to grab a chicken.

The day began as normal with Cockerel greeting the rising sun. Bob opened his eyes and peeped out from his kennel, he sniffed the air and his flop-ears twitched as he listened for the sounds of the world. He stood up and stretched his sleepy body then left his kennel and trotted over to the stable door, which was still closed, then he wandered over to the trees by the stream and left his mark against the trunk of an old oak that hung tight against the steep banks leading down to the babbling water.

Then he froze...

His nose picked up a faint scent. His ears twitched left and right as he sought for any unusual sounds. He heard the faint noises coming from the kitchen and his stomach grumbled. He heard the distant sound of a tractor in a field. He heard the horses chatting to each other inside the stables. From the coop came no sound. The chickens were quiet. The cockerel was quiet.

It had stopped its morning greeting.

Bob sniffed the air, wondering where the strange smell was coming from then, all of a sudden, the chicken coop erupted in squawks and shrieks and the fluttering of wings. Without a second thought Bob turned and ran swiftly toward the coop, barking loudly as he ran as fast as a small brown dog can run, faster over a short distance than any of the big dogs of the hunt, faster than the Big Man's hounds, Brian and Boru, he ran faster across the yard than either Mercy or Cannon, the Big Man's horses, could have ran. He ran as fast as he could because it was his Main Job to guard the hen coop. And the hen coop was under attack!

In a matter of moments Bob skedaddled around the corner just in time to see a small, reddish-brown shape with a bushy tail escaping through a fresh gap in the chicken wire that guarded the coop. Bob had never seen Mr. Fox close up, he was only a young dog after all, but he knew a mortal enemy when he saw one, and he gave chase with loud barks.

Reynard the Fox ran straight and true toward the distant fence, his short legs a blur of movement, and only the fact that he held a squawking chicken in his jaws slowed him down. He heard a bark from behind him and glanced back to see a small, feisty brown dog giving chase. 'Drats!', he thought, gripping the noisy chicken tighter, "Double drats!', he thought again, 'I've been spotted.'

He heard another bark, closer still, and he knew that carrying the chicken he would never escape, so he dropped the struggling bird and kept on running. The chicken landed in a heap and flew straight into the air, clucking and shouting with its chicken voice. Bob sped straight past it, intent on catching that horrid Mr. Fox who had dared enter his territory. The fox, older and wiser than Bob, ran down to the brook and across the babbling waters, then up the other side, then around a bend, then down to the stream again and this time he ran along the course of the shallow running water for fifty yards until he came to another bend, at which point he left the stream and ran upwards towards a copse of trees. Bob followed him down and through the stream and up the slope, then lost him when the fox's trail disappeared back down into the running water. His barking stopped being one of sheer anger and became a cry of 'Be off!' mixed with growls of frustration. Eventually he had to give up the chase.

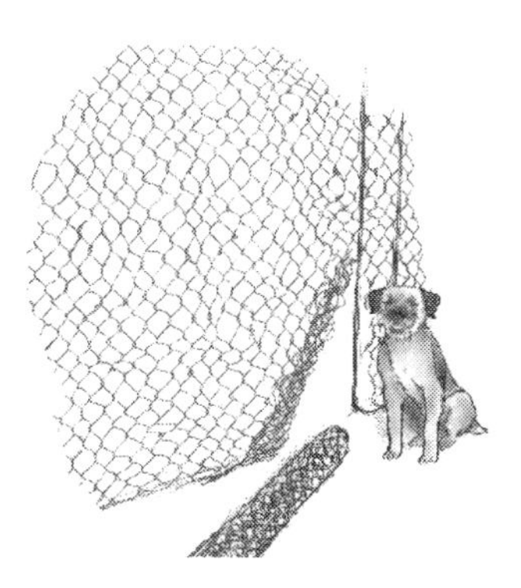

But Bob was not giving up the hunt. He returned to the coop, where the almost-stolen chicken had returned and where the cockerel had taken up his morning doodle-dooing and he lay down at the damaged fence and kept guard.

Bob's Adventure

The very next morning, after breakfast, and after he had watched Stan the Stableboy fix the hole in the coop fence, Bob went out on patrol, determined to find out where Mr. Fox had gone. After some time, near the young copse, he picked up the faint scent and his nose twitched, his ears listened left and right, and he followed the scent for a mile or two until he came to the main road. The Girl always told him not to cross the main road. But the Girl also told him he must always guard the chicken coop, and that was his Main Job, so Bob carefully crossed the main road, though the blaring horn from a large truck that swept by made him leap into the air, and he dashed to the other side with a fast-beating heart, slipped through the hedge, and found himself at the edge of a ploughed field.

He began to sniff around for traces of Mr. Fox. After a few minutes he found the smell again, it was a little stronger here, and there were clear signs of digging where Mr. Fox had unearthed a family of field mice from beneath the hedge and eaten them all up. Bob looked around, he could see a man in the middle of the field, so he trotted over to say Hello! But despite Bob's clear greeting, the man didn't seem to see him, so Bob circled him once or twice, but the man neither looked nor moved. Bob loved people, and people loved Bob but this man just stood there, in the middle of the field, saying nothing. Suddenly a small bird peeped out from beneath the man's hat. 'Who are you?' the bird cheeped in its high, clear voice.

'I'm Bob. I live in the Big House.'

'Why are you in this field, so far from the Big House?' the bird asked, fluttering its wings so that it perched on the brim of the hat. Bob realised the standing figure wasn't a man. He'd heard people call this thing a stare-crow because, he thought, it just stared at crows. And stared across fields.

'Do you live in the stare-crow?' Bob asked.

'I live here with my chicks and my wife. She is out in the fields looking for food.'

'I get food from Stan the Stableboy, or from the kitchen,' Bob said.

The bird didn't know Stan. He didn't know what a kitchen was. 'What are you looking for?' he asked Bob.

'I'm looking for Mr. Fox. He tried to steal chickens from the coop. I'm going to catch him.'

The bird didn't know what a coop was, but he knew Mr. Fox.

'He walked past the corner of the field this morning,' the bird cheeped. 'He ate some field mice. What are you going to do when you find him?'

'I'm going to bark at him,' Bob said. 'And chase him far away.'

'What will you do if he doesn't run away?' the little bird asked.

'I will bite him until he does,' Bob said. 'I am only a little brown dog but I have very big teeth for my size.' He bared them to show the bird who chirruped in fright and said,

'Don't eat me!'

'I don't eat birds,' Bob said, 'But I do chase foxes.'

'How far will you chase him?' the bird asked.

'As far as it takes to catch him,' Bob said. And with that he set off in search of Mr. Fox.

Back at the Big House, no one had yet missed Bob. Stan was busy cleaning the horses, Mrs. Hands was preparing lunch, the Butler was polishing the silverware, Old Tom was pruning tomato bushes and the Big Man was in his office doing the books. Celia was far away, still at school, sitting behind a desk, wishing she was at home, wishing she was walking across the fields with Bob. Only one more day until half term, she thought, then I can go home and see father and

Bobby. Her heart tugged with longing and missing them both. With a sigh, she turned away from staring out of the window and back to her schoolwork.

At the very same moment that Celia was sighing wistfully at her desk, Bob was doggedly following the scent of Mr. Fox across fields, fallow and ploughed. The sun was high in the sky and the wind was soft and Bob was proud of his mission. He stopped to drink water from a brook. 'I've never been here before,' he realised. 'I feel a little bit tired.' But when he'd drank his fill he felt better, and carried on tracking Mr. Fox, and a while later he came to a narrow bridge that seemed to hang over a wide, shallow river. Mr. Fox had come this way so Bob followed him across the bridge. He didn't know it, because these things don't matter to dogs in general, or Border Terriers in particular, and anyway, the soldiers and kings kept changing the maps, but Bob had just crossed the official border from England into Scotland. And yet, somehow, despite not knowing that particular fact, the air felt different somehow, and Bob could feel the change.

A little while later he came to a rough path that turned off the road and led into a pine forest where the trees were so close-packed that when he entered, the sky turned darker, the air became cooler, and Bob had been walking for hours - it suddenly seemed that the day was almost over.

Bob was tired now.

And very hungry.

But Bob was also a Border Terrier, and he knew he had to chase Mr. Fox so far that Mr. Fox never dared return to the Big House. Presently he came to a low cottage, nestled into the south side of a low hill, where the trees were thinner and the path clearer. The cottage smelled of smoke from the chimney, cooked food from the kitchen, and clean washing that hung from the line. It felt very homely. He trotted up to the gate and stopped when a gruff voice asked

'Who are you?'

'I'm Bob,' he told the owner of a voice, a dog that appeared at the other side of the gate. This dog had a squashed face and rolls of skin on his neck and shoulders. His body was very chunky and his legs were short and wide set. 'Are you a... dog?' Bob asked, unsure.

'I'm the king of dogs,' the ugly dog told him. 'I'm a bulldog.'

'What's a bulldog?'

'We're the kings of dogs. We eat bulls,' the ugly dog said, as though it was obvious.

'How many bulls have you et?' Bob asked.

'None yet, but as soon as I get a chance...' and the ugly dog growled and opened his mouth to show his intent. Bob saw his wide, wide mouth and felt sure that if any dog could eat a bull, this dog could. 'I'm called Edward,' the ugly dog said.

'Have you got any food you could spare?' Bob asked. 'I'm hungry.'

'I might have,' Edward growled.

'But you're probably too busy chasing bulls to worry 'bout me,' Bob said.

'I most certainly am,' Edward's voice was so low it seemed to grumble, 'But I can probably spare a sausage or two. Come with me.' Edward turned to walk away and Bob waited a bit then squeezed between the bars of the gate and followed him. Border terriers have large teeth but narrow shoulders, so they are good for squeezing into small places, like fox dens and garden gates. When they got to the back of the house, Edward paused then gave a short bark.

'Wuff!' he said.

Bob barked too – Wuff! - but Edward told him, 'Barking is my job,' so Bob stopped barking and waited. Edward barked again, then the door opened and a little old lady peered out.

'Are you hungry again Edward?' she asked in a thin, wavering voice, and Edward barked. She turned to look at Bob. 'Oh, you've found a friend. Who is this?' she said, and asked Bob, 'Would you like a sausage too?' Bob barked, he couldn't help it, he was very hungry, then he glanced at Edward and thought, *oops*, but Edward said nothing, and the old lady went back inside to fetch sausages for the two of them speaking almost to herself, 'Well, it *is* almost teatime.'

After a tremendous feast of two sausages and a crumbled biscuit followed by a large drink from Edward's water bowl, Bob settled down on the front step of the homely cottage in the woods, next to Edward. 'Thankyou for letting me eat part of your meal,' Bob said.

'The king of dogs will always share his meal,' Edward said. Then he said, 'It does get a little lonely sometimes. Would you like to stay here with me?'

Bob said, 'I am very grateful for the offer but I am chasing Mr. Fox and can't stop until I catch him.'

Edward nodded sagely. 'It is the same when a bulldog catches a bull, we grab it by the nose do not let go until we are triumphant.' Then he said, 'I do believe a red fox passed nearby earlier today. It was heading west, towards the setting sun'

'Really?' Bob said. Well I must be off, thanks again!' and with that he turned stood and stretched, and licked Edward's ear, then he trotted back to the gate, squeezed between the iron bars and set off west, towards the setting sun.

Towards Mr. Fox.

Sometime later it was growing dark and Bob, though he would never give up chasing Mr. Fox, had to admit he was a little bit tired. The sausages from Edward and the old lady had been lovely but it was all he'd eaten all day and he missed his kibbles from Stan the stableboy.

The sky was growing dark blue and Bob looked up to see the stars in the sky. He knew each star in the sky contained the spirit of every Border Terrier that had lived and worked and been happy, and they looked down on the world and watched over little brown dogs like him. He knew this because The Girl had told him. He paused to drink some water from a ditch. Then he followed the ever-fainter scent of Mr. Fox.

Later still and it had grown very dark. Bob thought he should find a sheltered spot to sleep. He would take up the hunt in the morning. He could smell rain in the air and he needed a sheltered spot somewhere out of the weather. The grey clouds were already beginning to block out the stars. He trotted along the narrow lane looking for a spot. Then a very fortunate thing happened.

As the first spot of rain dropped heavily from the sky and onto Bob's nose, in the distance Bob saw a faint light, and he smelled the comforting scents of man and horse and dog. So he trotted on until he came to the strangest little house he had ever seen. It was not much longer than the horse that stood in front of it, it had a wheel at each corner and a little chimney on top of the roof from which the smoke of a cooking fire drifted. The house had round walls and was painted lots of different colours.

'Hello,' said the horse.

'Hello Mr. Horse,' I'm Bob,' Bob replied.

'Hello Bob,' said the horse. 'My name is Toby. The man is inside.'

Bob trotted to the back of the little house on wheels and found a door. He barked, once. There was no reply, so he barked again. This time there was a scraping noise from inside and the little door at the back of the house creaked open and a strange little man peered out. He had a thin, wiry face and a long stubbly chin, on top of which was a small mouth that sheltered beneath the crag of a long, crooked nose. The small mouth seemed to be chewing something as it spoke. 'Whoosh there?' the mouth said.

Bob barked again.

'Oh,' said the little man looking down in surprise, 'Jingsh, theresh a wee dug!' The little man disappeared back into the little house then reappeared a moment later, chewing on something that made his mouth bigger. 'Come here, duggie,' the man said, beckoning.

Bob looked at the steps to the little door and barked again. The man looked down at the stairs too, 'Yon steers are a wee bit steep?' he asked, then stepped down from the little house. Bob saw that he was wearing slippers, a dressing gown decorated with stars and symbols, and a red velvet cap. The man bent down and pickup Bob up, and for all his small stature he was surprisingly strong and Bob felt safe that he wouldn't drop him as he carried him back up the wobbly wooden steps into the tiny, most crowded house Bob had ever seen.

The house contained only one room, and from the door at the back looking forwards it was filled with small pieces of machinery, then a tiny little stove and table, then a very comfortable looking sofa that ran the width of the home. It smelled of pipe-smoke and oil and lemon, and it smelled welcoming. The man put Bob down and closed the door. 'Rain's comin' he said to himself, then, 'Aye,' with a big sigh as he sat down on the sofa, and leaned against a furry black cushion.

The cushion opened an eye.

It was a dog.

'Hamish, Hamish,' the man said, 'Here's a wee frien' for you,' and Hamish, for that was the black cushion's name, uncurled himself from his sleeping position and sat up. Then he lay back down again and went to sleep.

Bob decided the best thing to do was for him to get comfortable too, so he stood and turned in a circle three times, then lay down on a comfy spot and fell fast asleep. He'd had a very busy day!

Early the next morning Bob woke from a long, comfortable sleep. His bed was soft and smelled nicely of dog and human and frying bacon.

Bacon?

He lifted his sleepy head and found that he was not snug in his kennel but instead was lying on a soft bed in a tiny room and he was watching a strange little man with a whiskery face frying bacon on a tiny stove. The man turned and said, 'You're awake, so I s'pose. Whid ye like a wee bit o' cracklin?'

Bob wasn't sure what cracklin was but he was sure it meant food so he licked his lips. The little old man took the bacon from the pan and cut it up into small pieces. He placed an equal share on two plates and put the plates on the floor.

Bob jump lightly down and stood by the plate. 'G'wan boy,' the old man said, 'eat up!'

Bob tucked in, munching down the bacon in a few gulps. As he paused to lick the plate he saw the little old man pick up the old dog from the bed where Bob had been lying and put him gently down by the other plate. The other dog was very old and Bob said, 'Hello again!'

'Whit?' said the old dog, who was a little bit deaf. Even though he had thick, black wiry hair he was grey around the muzzle, so Bob could tell he was very old.

'Hello!' Bob barked loudly.

The old dog ate his bacon slowly and Bob noticed he only had a few teeth left. When he was finished he too licked his plate and then, finally he said, 'Hello. I'm Hamish.'

'I'm Bob,' said Bob, loudly.

The old man had opened the door and Hamish trotted to the steps and waited until the man picked him up and carried him down to the ground. Bob went to the door and looked at the drop to the ground, then carefully stepped down the creaky wooden staircase until he was on the ground. He trotted round to see the horse, which had spent the night sleeping standing up and, Bob noticed, had been wearing a canvas coat and hood. He watched as the man unfastened the straps for the coat. The horse shook himself.

Bob waited a bit then said, 'Hello Toby!'

'Good morning Bob,' said Toby who was waiting patiently for the man to return with a bag of food, which he fastened to Toby's head. The man then turned to Bob and looked thoughtful. 'Weeeelll,' he said softly. 'I wonder you bide, wee duggie?' After staring at Bob for another moment or two he went back to the back of the tiny house and Bob followed. He scampered up the steps behind the man and sat on the mat watching as the small man opened a drawer, then closed it, then opened another and another until he eventually found what he was looking for. 'Here we are,' he said, finally, taking a leather wallet from the drawer and sitting down at his bed, which Bob saw had miraculously changed into a table and bench seat. The man sat down and opened the wallet. 'This is mah service book. My serial number' he pointed to some squiggles on the cover of the book. He spoke slowly, 'John James Tinkle, Corporal, number seven, oh, five, five, four, one, eight.' He paused, then said, 'Fifty-fifth, Regiment of Foot.' He smiled to himself, 'Aye' he said, his voice gentle. Bob watched him intently, wondering what he was doing. The man flicked through the pages until he found what he was looking for, a folded photograph which fell out onto the table. The man opened the photograph carefully and flattened it onto the bench. He studied it for a few moments, then looked carefully at Bob, then back at the photograph. 'I wonder...?' the man said. Then his eyes perked up as the sound of Hamish barking for attention came from outside. 'Gimmy a meenit,' he said gently to Bob and went outside to carry Hamish inside. When he got back he closed the door and found Bob sitting on the bench looking at the wallet and the photograph. The man carefully set Hamish on the bench beside Bob and sat down again. Hamish glanced at Bob then laid his head on the man's leg and promptly went to sleep. The man looked at Bob and said, 'Hamish is gettin owld, he gets awfy tired.' Then he turned back to the photograph and repeated, 'I wonder...?'

Bob looked at the photograph. He could see shapes and shades of black and white but he couldn't recognise what the photograph was because doggy-eyes don't recognise pictures very well. If he had been able to see the photograph he would have seen a splendid company of soldiers in splendid uniforms, each man with a splendid moustache and one or two of them had splendid beards, and if he had really looked, he would have a seen a fine young man in a perfectly arranged uniform with a perfectly splendid moustache who looked exactly like a younger version of the old man who was sitting next to him. He would have seen that at the bottom of the photograph someone had written, *Mafeking, May 1900*. But the main thing Bob would have seen, if he could, was that of a tiny uniformed figure sitting proudly at the front of the middle row of men. This figure had four legs and a tail, he was smiling and his long canines showed white against the dun shades of his perfect little tunic, and he had the most splendid moustache and beard of all of them. And the most amazing thing Bob would have noticed, if he could have, was that the figure in the photograph looked the exact double of Bob himself. The little old man stroked Bob's fur as he studied the photograph. He glanced at Bob's tail and saw a white stripe and nodded, he looked at Bob's chest and saw a white blaze and said to himself, 'Aye.' He raked Bob's fur to check the wiry overcoat, then studied his narrow shoulders and deep chest. Finally, he folded the photograph and slotted it back inside the wallet. 'Whuar did ye come from, wee duggie? I wonder whuar ye bide?' Bob watched him as the man stood and carefully placed the wallet back into the drawer. He turned to Bob and said, 'I hev a wee idea. Aye, a wee idea.' He smiled at Bob and then stroked Hamish's muzzle. 'You twa wee dugs settle in. Ah've a bit o' work to do this morn.'

'Are ye ready?' Tinks asked the two dogs an hour later. Hamish replied by looking right then left, sitting as he was to the side of the little old man who occupied the middle space on the front bench seat of the little house on wheels. Bob sat on the other side and gave a little bark. The little old man flicked the reins and the horse gave a quiet whinny and set off, dragging the house behind it.

Bob sat on the bench next to the old man, watching the countryside as they passed, smelling the lovely smells of nature, his ears twitching at strange noises. Hamish sat on the other side, sleeping. Bob thought Hamish must be very old. He understood that old animals liked to sleep. Bob however liked to be awake to experience the strange sounds and smells. He felt very comfortable sitting on the bench, but he also missed his kennel at the side of the Big House. He thought of the Girl and gave a little whimper and the little old man, as if understanding his thought, stroke his head. 'Nivver fret, wee duggie. Wha'll get yer hame soon enough, aye.'

Bob was comforted by the tone of the man's voice, though he struggled to understand the exact words. People didn't speak like animals, with their bodies and their tails and their facial expressions, they made strange sounds and they didn't move around when they talked. But they were kind to Bob and he loved them, so he put up with their strange sounds and ways of talking.

Bob sat on the bench enjoying the ride as the countryside rolled slowly past. As the sun rose higher into the sky they reached a small village of grey-stone houses and shops with sparkling windows. The little old man stopped the little house and leapt nimbly from his seat. Bob looked around then carefully jumped down to join him, and watched as the man pulled a bench from beneath the body of the little house. He then fastened a series of wheels to the table and pushed it out into the street. From beneath the table he took a silver disc and a small hammer, which he banged loudly, making Bob jump and bark with alarm. The little old man kept banging and after a few minutes a lady appeared at a nearby doorway, then disappeared, then reappeared again, bringing a tray with her.

'Good morning Tinks,' the lady said. 'I'm so pleased you're here. My knives are so very blunt!'

'Ah'll fix them in a smidge, Missus Wilson,' he said in reply.

The woman placed the tray on his table and, sitting at a tiny stool, the little old man took the first knife from the tray, held it against a disk and, with his feet tapping up and down, the disc began to spin. He held the edge of the knife against the wheel and it made a grinding noise as sparks flew off. Bob gave another bark and Mrs. Wilson asked, 'Is this your new dog, Tinks?'

'No, he's jis' a lodger. We're taking him hame.'

Tinks took each knife in turn and ground it against the spinning stone wheel. After a while Bob became used to the noise and learned to ignore it. He didn't like the sparks, so while Tinks was busy he wandered off to sniff the flowers. When he looked back he saw there was a queue of people waiting for Tinks to grind their knives against the spinning wheel. Bob thought humans were strange. They did strange things. He loved people but he didn't quite understand them. They didn't sniff or leave their mark against trees, and they didn't always like it when he licked them. He heard one man say, 'By Tinks, my razor was so blunt! The customers were complaining.'

And Tinks said, 'Man the edge has rolled: ah'll need to grind it away and resharpen it. You'll be trimming hair in a jiffy.'

Yes, Bob thought as he watched, people were very strange.

After a while the queue died down and Tinks completed his job. Bob sat on the grass watching as the little old man put away the wheels and the little bench. He looked around and clicked his tongue, which Bob knew was a sign for Ready! so he trotted over and followed Tinks up onto the front bench. 'I've made some chinks,' Tinks said, jingling a soft bag full of little coins. 'Let's away tae the market.' And with that he picked up the reins, gave a little flick, and the horse began to pull the little home away, out of the village and into the countryside.

A long, long way away, in the far south of the country, at a tiny train station, a little girl was sitting on her suitcase at the end of the platform. She was wearing her school uniform frock and blazer, and a straw hat to protect her from the sun, and she quietly hummed a tune to herself. In her satchel she had a packed lunch and a bottle of lemonade. She was thinking of home, of seeing her daddy, and Cook, and Stan the Stableboy. And she thought especially of seeing her lovely Border Bear. In the nearby fields she could see butterflies and bees and it made her think of Bob. 'Bobbee,' she whispered quietly. 'I'll see you soon.'

And at that very same moment, in stables by the Big House, Stan the Stableboy was very worried. There was no sign of Bob. His kennel was cold and unslept in and his breakfast bowl uneaten. It was not unknown for Border Terriers to get trapped underground in rabbit warrens and fox dens and Stan was extremely concerned. 'Oh Bob,' Stan said to himself. 'Where *have* you got to?'

An hour later, the little old man was steering his horse-drawn caravan into the little town, through the market-day crowds and past the noisy motor cars and charabancs and parked neatly in a little slot between two rows of barrows and stalls where people stood and sold everything from fruit to jam to cushion covers, to pork loins and sausages, reconditioned watches and clocks, second-hand clothes, knitwear and children's booties, fish on ice slabs, rusted bicycles, almost-new bicycles, pies, peas, pies *and* peas, and everything else that can be sold or ever has been sold in a small market town on the borders of England and Scotland. As Tinks stepped down from the caravan the clock struck twelve times. Bob thought this was a strange sound but he ignored it and, drawn by the smell of sausages, he leapt down from the front seat of the caravan and disappeared between the legs of the crowds of people in the search for food. And as Bob trotted happily between stall, sniffing and licking and occasionally snaffling a small, dropped piece of food, Tinks was setting up again.

But this time he was not sharpening knives and cutlery. After Bob had done a full circuit of the market square, found and eaten an almost complete sausage *and* a juicy pie crust, he returned to find Tinks dressed in a purple velvet jacket and blue felt cap covered in tiny stars, sitting on a little stool, playing stirring music on a huge old accordion. People smiled, one or two shuffled their feet in time to the music, and some people dropped money into a little mahogany box as they passed. The nearby stallholders stood and watched, drinking tea from tin cups. Tinks played on, now a happy tune to dance to, and now a sad, lonely tune of moors and battles lost and wounded warriors. There was a pause as Tinks tuned up his accordion, and then he began to sing a song in his high, wavering voice, of love-lost and broken hearts and magical places. The music was sad and plaintive and can't be copied down onto this page here, but if you were to listen to the words, they'd sound something like this:

Noo haway all ye laddies ahv a tale to tell

An al tell yes all aboot it if ye keep it to yoursel

By a wee muckle bridge forty miles from Troon

There's a seecrit heilan village by the name o Brigadoon

Brigadoon Brigadoon

Brigadoon Brigadoon

Al dance wi ye all day but the evenin comes twae soon

When ye wake up in the morning yel be lonely fir a loon

And the lasses all away, Brigadoon, Brigadoon

Noo this heilan village has a secret to tell

But they share it oot with nae-one and they keep it tae themsel

For the village only wakes once a hundred years

And the lassies dance all day for the hearts tae break

And the loons walk yon roads and they hear thon tunes

And they find themselves a way for to find them Brigadoon

And they meet themselves a quinie and they dance with her to dawn

But when they wake next mornin they find Brigadoon has gone

Brigadoon Brigadoon

Brigadoon Brigadoon

Al dance wi ye all day but the evenin comes twae soon

When ye wake up in the morning yel be lonely fir a loon

And the lasses all away, Brigadoon, Brigadoon

Some say it's a curse, that the village hides away

And a loon may waste his life just to find it one mair day

For the lassie that he loves she has gone far away

And the village it lies sleepin in a far hideaway

Brigadoon Brigadoon

Brigadoon Brigadoon

Al dance wi ye all day but the evenin comes twae soon

When ye wake up in the morning yel be lonely fir a loon

And the lasses all away, Brigadoon, Brig a doon....

(Quinie is an old Highland word for a young lady of marriageable age.

Loon is the equivalent word for a young man of marriageable age)

Listening to this tune, Bob felt a sudden urge to join in, he couldn't help it, and even though he tried to stop it, there grew a low, rising howl at the back of his throat. As Tinks played his tune, Bob began to howl and yodel along with him. People stopped and listened, pointed and laughed, but Bob couldn't help himself, he howled and hiccupped and sang along to Tinks' tune.

When, finally, the tune ended, Bob's voice died away to a whimper and finally, silence. The entire market square seemed to have gone quiet. And then suddenly, ragged claps broke out amongst the crowd and everyone nearby clapped loudly. Tinks paused, then took a bow, and then gestured towards Bob at which point the people clapped even more.

'Jingsh, yer a clever wee duggie,' Tinker said as they traveled once more through the countryside, holding his little bag of coins that had grown even heavier from the money he made at the market. They rumbled over a little bridge that Bob recognised from the day before when he'd been chasing Mr. Fox. He suddenly remembered what he was supposed to be doing and he barked once, very loud, just in case any foxes or Hejogs were nearby. Hamish looked up from his sleep, yawned, and Tinks stroked his old black and grey muzzle for a minute, then Hamish put his chin on his paws and went fast asleep again.

At the Big House, Stan the Stableboy was now frantic with worry. Where was Bob? Would he be found before Celia returned? If he was lost... oh, the thought was too much to bear, so he increased his search, walking round the house and fields, trotting down to the brook, peering into the old copse, clicking his tongue, whistling and, all the time, listening for a clue as to where Bob might be. Old Tom the gardener watched Stan, as he did a circuit of the walled garden, he took off his cap and scratched his head, puzzled at the stableboy's behaviour. And far away, on a small, slow steam-train, in a compartment that smelled of tobacco and polished leather, Celia sat by herself gazing out of the window.

Earlier, the train had chugged past a number of huge cooling towers, then an hour or more ago they'd got to York, where she finished off her packed lunch and most of her lemonade. And now they were heading north. At that moment, the ticket inspector popped his head through the door. 'Durham in a minute, young miss, then Newcastle-Upon-Tyne, Alnmouth and on to Berwick-upon-Tweed, which is your stop, I believe.'

'Yes, thank you,' she said.

The ticket inspector smiled kindly and then closed the door, leaving her alone again.

Lord Craigmorley glanced at his watch.

He was an impatient man, always busy, always hurrying through the day, and standing at the front door of Craigmorley House taxed his patience. But wait he would, because his beloved daughter was due home in ten minutes. Hooks, the Butler, had driven to Berwick to collect her and by the Lord's calculation they should be home soon. He missed his daughter terribly, but he felt it was best that she went off to school. Craigmorley House was no place for a young lady to spend all her time, though when she was here he was filled with a gladness that he could not and would not ever show to anyone. He glanced across to where Stan stood, at the side of the house, looking worried. 'Where's Bob?' he shouted.

'I, er, I,' Stan stuttered.

Lord Craigmorley was about to say something else when suddenly, over the horizon and along the lane came a vehicle.

He watched it until it came properly into view. But it wasn't Hooks the Butler delivering his daughter from the station. It was a little old caravan, led by a little old horse, and on it sat a little old man. He watched as the caravan approached the gates and then crunched onto the gravel drive, halting when it reached the fountain, and he walked down off the step to greet it, wondering who it could be. And at that very moment, Hooks the Butler pulled up beside it in the car, and Celia climbed out.

Stan's heart was in his mouth and he couldn't quite understand what happened next because, as Celia climbed out of the car, from the tiny little caravan that was parked beside it, Bob suddenly appeared, leaping down from the front seat to rush gladly up to Celia and jump up and down in front of her until she knelt down and let him lick her and smell her and leap all over her. It wasn't until Lord Craigmorley stepped in and said, 'Enough Bob!' that little Bob calmed down enough to allow Celia to hug her father. Then, greetings over, Mrs. Hands the Cook was there to help Celia into the house with her suitcase and get her settled in.

Having watched her go into the house, Lord Craigmorley walked over to the little caravan and spoke to the little old man, who climbed down from his seat and stood erect in front of him. 'Corporal John Tinkle,' he said, formally, 'Fifty-fifth Regiment of Foot. At your service sir.'

Lord Craigmorley, who had been a Major in the Great War, returned the salute and said, 'At ease, Corporal.' Then he asked, 'How did you happen to have my daughter's terrier in your caravan?' and his voice was kind but he glanced darkly towards Stan as Tinks began to tell him the story.

It was later only when Hooks the Butler told Mrs. Hands the Cook, who mentioned it to Grace the kitchen maid, that Stan found out what had actually happened. Stan had taken a break from seeing to old Toby, the little man's horse that pulled the little man's caravan, and he was at the kitchen door eating a slice of apple pie.

'The little old man knew the Laird's faitha,' Grace said, her soft Scottish burr almost as welcome as the slice of apple pie she'd given him. 'They fought together in Africa, against the Boors.'

'The Boers,' Stan corrected, and she raised an eyebrow so he shut up again and ate his pie.

'Aye, weel,' she continued, 'The little old man recognised Bob because when the Awld Laird was in Africa fighting the Bo*ers*,' and she paused as she emphasised this word. 'The awld laird had a dug jis like Boab. So he thought perhaps

Boab belonged to Craigmorley.' She smiled sweetly, taking the empty plate from Stan, 'And he *dis*, so, lucky you!'

'Aye, lucky me,' Stan said, sheepishly. 'How on earth did Bob get that far away?'

'Wha knaws? But don't tell Celia, mark ye, if she thought he'd been lost she'd break her heart, even though he was found safe.' She smiled, 'That wee man is about to go, so I hope you've fed and cleaned his cuddy.'

Stan said, 'Yes, old Toby is clean, fed and rested. I'll go and get him hitched up.'

'Tubby,' she said. 'Funny name for a gallower.'

'Toby,' Stan almost corrected, but he didn't. He liked apple pie too much, and he quite liked Grace too. So instead, he left the kitchen door and went to the stable to fetch the old Toby and hitch him to the little old wagon.

Lord Alistair escorted Tinks out to his caravan where Toby stood in his harness, glossy-coated, well-fed and happy, and Hamish sat watching from the front step of the little carriage. 'You're always welcome to visit Craigmorley,' the Lord told Tinks.

'Aye, you're a grand man,' Tinks said, 'Jis lik' your faither.'

Lord Craigmorley smiled. He didn't often smile but two large drams and a good conversation with an old soldier was sufficient to put a smile on his face. He watched as Tinks climbed deftly into the front seat next to an old, black-coated, grey-muzzled Scotch terrier that appeared to be fast asleep, picked up the reins and clicked his tongue. Toby the horse gave a little neigh and took the strain as the little vehicle creaked and turned on the drive, heading for the gates and the open road. From an upstairs window Celia sat watching the scene, with Bobby on her lap. She stroked him as she watched the caravan leave the drive. 'What a strange little man,' she said to Bob. 'I wonder why he was here?'

Bob wanted to tell Celia about Mr. Fox and the Stare-crow and Edward the King of Dogs, he wanted to tell her about the cosy caravan that smelled of pipe smoke and lemon, and the busy market where he sang along to the sad music, he wanted to tell her about Sleepy Hamish the old dog who lived with the little old man. But he couldn't because, sadly, humans don't understand dog language. So he did what dogs do when they can't speak to humans, he nuzzled her with his wet nose.

'Bobbee,' she said, 'Bobbee *Bear*,' and she hugged him so tight that he squirmed and licked and nuzzled her even more.

'I am *so* glad to be home with you and daddy,' she told him as she hugged him. 'I love you both so very much.'

Bob was very happy to be with the Girl.

His Girl.

Because he loved her so very much too.

Bob saves the day

A few evenings after Celia had returned from school she was sitting quietly reading in living room. Daddy was reading too, and smoking his pipe, which she quite liked the smell of, but not too much. Bob was lying curled at her feet, feeling most content.

'What are you looking at, daddy?' she asked.

He looked up, and so did Bob, who was always alert. 'The old man who came the same day you returned. He has loaned me a photograph of my own father, when he was a soldier, from a long time ago.'

'Oh, can I have a look?'

'Come and sit beside me,' her daddy said, so she went over to the large armchair and squashed in beside him. He pointed out the soldiers with their splendid uniforms, and in the middle was a tall man with a dark beard. 'That's your grandfather, my father. This picture was taken in Africa at the beginning of the century. I was just a child at the time.'

Celia studied the photograph. 'That little old man gave you this?'

'He loaned it to me to take a copy, I have to give him it back the next time he comes to visit. There he is,' and he pointed to a slight but very splendid figure to the left of her grandfather.'

'Was grandfather a general?' she asked.

'He was a Colonel. He was in charge of a regiment of eight hundred men.'

He was about to explain more, but Celia was transfixed by the tiny figure at the front of the picture. 'That's... that's Bobbee!' and she gave a little squeal of delight.

'No, darling, but he *is* Bob's ancestor.'

'His grandfather?'

'Perhaps his grandfather's grandfather,' he said.

Celia studied the photograph more.

Daddy said, 'Our family have always had little brown dogs. Did you know that when the Romans came to Britain two thousand years ago they said the natives had small, feisty dogs that dug into the ground to catch vermin and barked alarm when visitors arrived. So even our ancestors had them.

And the Craigmorley family have always stuck with the same lineage of the breed, so that Bob is a descendent of my father's dog. He was also called Bob,' he added.

'Are all our dogs called Bobby, daddy?'

'No. When I was a child I had a little brown dog, but she was called Bess. The Bob you see on the photograph was Bess' older brother.'

'But we've always had little brown border bears?' she said, and Bob, who was listening, decided that the conversation was about him. He could tell by the way the Girl kept looking towards him and saying his name. He felt very proud.

'Yes. They're quick and brave and...'

'...and loving and caring,' she added.

Her daddy smiled. 'Yes, all of those things too.' He continued, 'Grandfather's Bob had lots of adventures. He was kidnapped by the Boers you know, then he lived with a Zulu tribe for some while and became a favourite of the Zulu King.

Eventually he was rescued when a missionary took a photograph of the tribespeople and Grandfather recognised him in the photograph. He brought him home in 1902 and they both lived a long happy life together in this very house.'

'I hope my Bobbee doesn't have adventures,' she said. 'I like him to be safe at home with me.'

'I hope so too,' Daddy said, 'but in a pinch, Bob would be a brave little fellow to have at your side.'

That night, after Celia tucked Bob into his kennel and said goodnight, Bob lay contentedly with his chin on his paws, watching the stars in the sky and sniffing the air until he fell into a deep sleep and dreamt he was a brave Roman soldier chasing rabbits across fields.

The very next morning, when Bob woke from his dreams in his cosy kennel, he got up and stretched, then yawned, then did his rounds as usual. He saw Stan at the door to the stables eating an apple, and watched for a while as he mucked out the horses, then he went around to sit and watch old Tom the gardener doing the weeding in the walled garden. Then he trotted down to the old copse by the stream, checked that the chickens were safe in their coop, because that was his Main Job, and then trotted back to the stable where Stan had put out a bowl of kibbles for him. He was satisfied that everything was as it should be and he was proud that he helped to look after the Big House.

An hour later he heard a noise at the kitchen door and went to investigate. He saw that the Girl was coming from the kitchen carrying a little knapsack and wearing sturdy walking clothes. 'Come on Bobbee!' she said brightly, 'we're going for a picnic.'

Bob didn't quite know what a picnic was but he smelled food in the knapsack, and he knew that he and the girl were going for a walk so he was very happy and he jumped up and down in excitement. Together they walked past the stables where Stan was grooming Mercy, one of the Big Man's horses.

'Where you two off, then?' he asked with a smile.

'We're going to walk up to the old priory for a picnic,' she told him.

Stan paused and said, 'Well mind you don't go through Miller's Field. Old Angus the bull is in there and he's not friendly. I took Mercy for a run last week and he chased us. Good job Mercy can leap a five-bar gate!'

'We aren't going through that field. We're going to walk past and along the lane until we get to the Barrows, then turn left towards the river.'

'Better watch the Barrow Wights don't get you!' Stan said, and pulled a face but Celia replied sternly that everyone knew Barrow Wights hadn't been seen in the north for nearly four hundred years.

They left Stan grooming the horses, walked past the chicken coop, now securely netted and safe from Mr. Fox, and along towards the old copse, then they walked up the hill and found the deep lane that wound along the edges of the river, sometimes going inland, sometimes passing so close to the river's edge that if you took a wrong step you might fall right in. After a while the lane ran away from the river and there were two or three fields away from the cool shade of the trees that overhung the running water. 'This is Miller's Field,' Celia told Bob, 'We will not go in there because Old Angus the Bull is in that field.'

Bob darted to the gate and saw, in the distance, a huge creature. It was red-coloured with a shaggy coat, and it had curved horns on the top of its head. Bob wished that Edward, the King of Dogs, could see Angus because he knew that Edward would grab the bull by the nose and hang on until he was victorious. 'Come on Bobbee!' Celia shouted from up the lane, so he turned and scampered after her, his tail wagging happily.

Eventually they came to a turn in the road. 'That's where the Barrows are,' Celia told him solemnly. 'In the old days, when the Reivers lived here, the Barrow Wights would come out at night and steal their children. They were the ghosts of kings from the days long before the Romans came and they have chain armour that clanked and long swords that shone in the dark.'

Bob barked.

'But I'm not scared,' she told him, 'Our family have always had little brown dogs to protect us.' Bob barked again and she giggled and together they ran swiftly past the gate, beyond which the old mounds of earth hosted the spirits of long dead kings.

Finally, they reached another path that led down towards the river again, where it ran wide and flat, to where the ruins of an old Abbey stood, the bare sandstone walls yellow-bright in the sunshine. Celia found a spot to leave her knapsack then they went for a scout around the abbey.

Finding nothing unusual apart from a huge cobweb inside the ruined chapel, they walked down to the riverbank and Celia threw sticks into the water and watched them flow away.

Bob grew bored of sticks so he trotted up to the meadow and chased butterflies though he did not manage to catch any. Eventually Celia came to collect him and they returned to the knapsack.

'I am very thirsty,' Celia said and opened the small lemonade bottle and took a drink. 'You must go to the river for a drink,' she told Bob, but he sat and panted and looked at her with sad eyes until she poured a little drop of lemonade into the mug she had brought, and then watched as he drank it. She took off her hat and tried to put it on his head, but he barked and grabbed the hat and ran around with it, ribbons flowing behind him, while she sat and laughed at his antics. Then she opened her knapsack and set out the little cloth and then opened the tuckbox. Then she carefully opened a little box that contained Bob's kibbles and poured them onto a flat stone so that they lay in a heap for about four seconds, until Bob returned, dropping the hat and trotting over swiftly to eat them all up. At the same time, she took out her sandwich and began to munch on it. Altogether, it was a very satisfactory meal, after a long walk on a sunny day in an ancient part of the country so, when they were finished, it was not unnatural that both girl and dog fell sound asleep in the shade of an old priory tower, built eight hundred years earlier (and mostly destroyed four hundred years after that). It was a lovely warm day and both were very tired after their adventures.

'Wake up Bobbee!' Celia said suddenly. Bob opened his eyes and stood up, stretching his spine. 'We've fallen asleep and it's late. We will have to get home.' She looked up at the sky and saw the sun was now hiding behind dark rainclouds. 'It's going to rain,' she told him. 'We will have to hurry or we will be soaked.' So they stood and dusted themselves off, Celia packing her knapsack and fastening it onto her back, then set off quickly back the way they came. But they couldn't outrun the clouds and after no more than ten minutes it began to rain, not heavy at first, but big drops, enough to wet them through. 'Let's take a shortcut,' Celia said, more to herself than to Bob, and together they climbed a gate (Bob darted between the bars) and ran across a field. Celia glanced to her right and saw, quite nearby, three mounds that lay in the field. Each mound alone was at least the size of the stables at Craigmorley and she knew they were the barrows. She didn't believe Stan, when he said that the Wights still lingered in the mounds, but the rain was heavier now, and the clouds and the dull light made the mounds appear ever so slightly threatening, and she didn't wish to hear the clanking of mail armour or see the dull glow of ancient longswords, so together they ran fast until, when they had climbed another gate, she had to stop and get her breath. Bob felt very wet but he was not tired. He waited until the Girl stood up straight and used the ribbons to fastened her bonnet tight over her head. 'Come on Bobbee,' she said, a determined note in her voice. 'We'll cut across this field then we're nearly home.'

The rain was very heavy now and both were soaked through as Celia clambered over the iron gate. She didn't notice it was padlocked and even if she had, she was too wet to wonder why, but even as Bob slipped between the bars of the gate he could sense danger and he began to bark loudly and dance round Celia's legs, a worried look on his face.

'Bobbee!' she said, 'Be quiet! We must get home!' It was raining heavy now, large drops fell on them like beats on a drum. At that very moment there was a crash of lightning and the fiery bolt struck a tree in the next field, splintering branches and sending up a shower of sparks and a pall of smoke. Celia shrieked and Bob barked even more, but then with a determined set to her chin she hurried across the field, now puddled by the drenching rain. Bob followed her, he didn't like lightning, it made his heart beat fast and it made him bark uncontrollably, but he followed the Girl, because protecting her was his Main Job, he knew that very much. And in the middle of the rain-storm, with the second crash of lightning, he heard something else, a rhythmic rumble of hooves approach. He glanced over his shoulder to see a huge red bull racing towards them. They were in Millers Field, he realised, and this was Angus the angry red bull!

Bob barked repeatedly until Celia, running now with her head down against the rain, turned to look and saw Angus, no more than thirty feet behind them, with the safety of the far gate at least twice that distance away. She shrieked again, with fear more than shock this time and ran faster towards the gate. Bob ran with her but when he turned his head he saw that the huge bull would run them down before they made the safety of the far gate. He wished Edward the King of Dogs was here. He would grab the bull by its nose until he was victorious.

Grab the bull by the nose!

Bob suddenly knew what he had to do, he knew he had to protect the Girl. He had to grab the bull by the nose! Grab it - don't be scared - he told himself, and with a feisty snarl, he turned and leapt at the charging bull, meeting it head on, his long teeth gripping onto the bull by its large soft nose. The bull roared and swerved to one side, shook its head one way, then the other, then it ran in circles bellowing as Bob hung on to its nose, growling in both fear and anger, how dare this bull threaten the Girl! And even as he saw for a brief moment, lit by a flash of lightning, Celia make the safety of the gate, the huge creature gave an almighty shake and Bob lost his grip and flew through the air like a bullet out of a gun. The world spun and spun, he heard Celia scream, and then he hit the ground with a thump and then the world went dark and he could not remember anything at all.

A Happy Ending

'Well, I think he'll be alright.'

Bob felt warm and cosy. Everything was dark. He wondered if he had become another star in the sky, if he had joined the other little dogs who twinkled and looked down on the world, keeping it safe. But the voice said, 'He's had rather a knock, but he's a tough little fellow.'

Bob opened an eye.

He was lying on a soft blanket in a room with the curtains drawn. His nose told him that Celia was nearby. He heard the Big Man say, 'She said he saved her. He grabbed Old Angus by the nose and gave her time to escape from the field.'

The other voice, kindly and older laughed and said, 'I'll have to tell old Mrs. Twine about that one. She has a bulldog called Edward. They live just across the way.' (Across the way means across the border). 'I bet Edward would have loved to have a pop at that big old bully.'

'Well, Bob did exactly that.'

'They're a great breed, Border Terriers,' the kindly voice said. 'Loving and gentle, but fearless.'

'This little fellow certainly is,' the Big Man said.

'What did the doctor say about Celia?'

'A week's bed rest and good food. She caught quite a chill.'

'Well, I recommend the same for your little fellow there, and don't let him run too much on that leg. It's not broken but it's badly knocked about. He'll let you know when he's ready.'

'Righto,' said the Big Man. 'Mrs. Hands said she's going to cook him a mince pie.'

Bob perked up, raising his head.

'Ah, he speaks English,' the kindly old man said.

'He speaks mince pie,' the Big Man said, 'Don't you, Bob?' and he rubbed Bob's head very gently.

Bob felt movement next to him and looked the other way where he saw Celia, tucked in bed. 'And how are you, little miss?' the man asked. 'Has the doctor fixed you?'

'Yes, thank you,' she said, feeling a little sorry for herself. 'I have a chill.'

'Running around in a thunderstorm will do that,' her father said. His voice was stern but he had a twinkle in his eye.

Bob snuggled up closer to The Girl, feeling her warmth against him. He felt proud that he had saved her because, even if protecting the chicken coop was his main job, protecting Celia was his Most Important job, and lying on her bed made him very happy, even if his leg was painful and his head thumped when he moved it.

'Well, Higson, thanks for your help,' the Big Man said to the kindly older man. 'This makes a change from you examining my horses.'

'He's a lovely little beastie,' he said, and this time Bob decided he didn't mind being called a beastie. 'The least I can do is make sure he's alright. But how on earth did you find them? It was quite a storm.'

'We can thank Stan for that. I was out walking the big lads,' (he meant Brian and Boru, the huge Irish Wolfhounds), 'so I didn't know they'd gone for a picnic. But as soon as the clouds grew heavy, Stan saddled Mercy and went to look for them. Most horses would bolt in a thunderstorm but Mercy is brave and young Stanley is a natural rider. He found Celia hugging Bob, trying to carry him through the rain, soaked to the skin. Picked them both up with one scoop it seems, and hurried home.'

'So Celia tried to carry her injured dog home in a thunderstorm?'

'She did.'

'Brave girl. There's quite a bond between them. And of course, the stable boy's a hero.'

'The stable boy's a fool at times, but yes, this time he was a hero. I'm very grateful to him.'

There was a pause and the man said, 'They're a pair, these two. You know, I think the best thing for them is a few days spent together to recuperate.'

'I think you're right the Big Man said,' and Bob heard the door open as the two men left the room.

Bob felt Celia's hand stroking his head gently, as though she knew he was feeling very sore and tender. 'Bobbee,' she whispered. 'My Border Bear...' and with that, and knowing the vet had said Bob would be fine, Celia fell into a deep, restful sleep. Bob lay quiet, listening to her breathing. He loved Celia's voice and he loved being near to her, and her scent was his favourite thing in the world. Well, he thought, apart from Mrs. Hands' mince pies.

He settled into a cosy spot on the bed.

All things considered, he thought, as he snuggled deeper into the cosy comfort of the bed, despite the bruises and the knocks, he was at that moment, a very, *very* content little dog.

Well, boys and girls, we will leave this brave little dog and his best human companion to rest and recover. But don't worry, Border Bob will return soon.

In the meantime... Ssshhhhhh!

More Border Bob stories coming soon:

Border Bob and Friends

Border Bob's Christmas

Boer Bob

Border Bob goes to war